Road to the Fire's Heart

a Firehawks romance story
by
M. L. Buchman

Buchman Bookworks

Other works by M.L. Buchman

Angelo's Hearth

Where Dreams are Born
Where Dreams Reside
Maria's Christmas Table
Where Dreams Unfold
Where Dreams Are Written

Deities Anonymous

Cookbook from Hell: Reheated
Saviors 101

Thrillers

Swap Out!
One Chef!
Two Chef!

SF/F Titles

Nara
Monk's Maze

1

Squinting her eyes didn't help.

"Driving through pea soup would be easier."

As usual, Trent made no comment. Instead, he leaned closer to the wheel and also squinted out at the wildfire's thick smoke. He was trying to turn strong-silent type into a lifestyle as if that was a good thing. He also didn't deal well with abstract things like metaphors. He was a reliable enough partner, just not the most flexible.

A decent enough person, just kind of clueless and…such a guy. Despite his being two years older than her, she'd taken to thinking of herself as his big sister, taking care of him when he was being particularly ridiculous or pitiable without his even realizing it. His fire skills were good, so she didn't have to fix that, he was simply a social train wreck and needed a bit of a buffer from the world at large.

Jill Conway-Jones looked back out the windshield of their heavy-duty Type 4 wildfire engine—the big truck was only a year old and still shone despite her and Trent driving to several fires already this season. She wished she knew more about paintings so that she could say one of those educated sounding phrases about how the raging, fiery hell was so awful that only Matisse could have done it justice. But even as she thought it, she knew it was wrong. Her best friend from childhood was the hotshot New York City artist. Jill was just a hotshot.

Actually, that's what she wanted to be. At the moment she was a wildland firefighter and engine driver lost deep in the Cascade wilderness of who-knew-where central

Washington. A wildfire engine driver, but it wasn't even her turn to drive. Trent was at the wheel and all she could do was try to figure out where they were.

US Forest Service fire road FS-273E was invisible, if that's what they were still on. Smoke was pouring across the road in thick black billows. Showers of brilliant orange sparks lit ash swirls from within as they blew by in vast clouds like the Monarch butterflies she'd once seen rising from a field of milkweed—a cloud of orange and black so thick that they seemed to block the sun.

Not that the sun was still aloft. She double-checked her watch, sunset should still be purpling the sky, but being deep within the steep mountains to all sides and the heavy smoke filling the valley, it was full night here. Wherever here was.

The headlights punched only a few feet into the smoke before reflecting back like high beams in fog.

They'd left the Stehekin River Valley Road what seemed hours ago. They were supposed to be delivering their seven

hundred and fifty gallons of water to a be-
leaguered crew high up on Tolo Mountain.
The one-lane dirt track had meandered up
into the hills. The road's edge was sometimes
carved out by rushing streams and at
other times the entire lane was blocked by
fallen trees. More than once they'd had to
stop, pull out their chainsaws, and chop
up eighty feet of flaming tree so that they
could tug it out of the way with the truck's
winch.

There was no turning around. No spot
in the road to do so even if the hotshot
crew hadn't needed their water. The wildfire engine was the only ground vehicle
with a chance of making it out to them.
The front cab looked like one of those
heavy-duty delivery trucks and had the big
growling diesel engine to match. The rear
had slab sides covered with doors for tools
and supplies. On the main bed was three
tons of water and twice the firehose that
any city firetruck could carry. They could
even drive slow along a fire's perimeter and
pump at the same time, a wildfire engine
specialty that no city engine could match.

Jill loved this machine for its raw brute strength, but still wanted to test herself against the fire with the Interagency Hotshot Crews—the IHCs were the elite wildfire fighters, along with the smokejumpers, and she wanted to be a part of that.

Trent was hugging the cliff to her right on the inside edge of the lane, which was all they could do. After the third time a branch had slapped her rearview mirror flat against the side of the engine, she gave up readjusting it. Opening the window invariably filled the cabin with smoke and there wasn't anyone crazy enough to be behind them anyway.

Jill looked up at the cliff and tried to see any dips or ridges. Maybe by the topography she'd be able to locate some similar shape on the map spread across her lap.

Then she saw it coming toward her. She barely had time to scream—

"Log!"

—before the tree tumbled down the hill and slammed into the side of the engine. It was three feet in diameter and at least thirty feet long. And it was alive with flame down its entire length.

The tree slammed into the engine and knocked it sideways as if it weighed nothing. The Type 4 engine weighed eight tons. Between fuel, the water, and crew, the engine was loaded with an extra five tons. Despite all of their mass and the grip of the rear dualies, they were swept sideways across the road like a dust bunny trying to escape a flaming broom.

They tumbled off the other side of the road. Even as they rolled down the steep slope, she could see Trent trying to steer. At the moment they were upside down, the engine roaring; he must also be trying the gas.

Jill nearly strangled when the throttle-hold of adrenaline fear clamped her throat closed at the same moment she had the urge to giggle. The image of the truck lying on its back and waving its little four-wheel drive in the air wouldn't go away even as the cab's roof crumpled dangerously low making them both duck.

The engine continued to roll, one side per panicked gasp until she was nearly hyperventilating. Once right side up, the spinning tires slammed them forward only for a second. The engine stalled hard then they continued once more onto their back with a resounding crash.

They finally came to a rest with the driver's side door down.

She dangled above Trent, suspended by her seatbelt.

"Nice driving there, Ace." It was either laugh or scream, and she struggled to avoid the latter.

Trent didn't answer. Nor did he offer one of his trademark grunts.

Ahead of them, out the shattered windshield, there was nothing but the pitch dark of night. There was light coming in through the back window—dark, orange light that flickered ominously. She twisted around to look. The massive burning log lay in the back of the engine, at least one end of it. It was still burning which only added to the bad. Looking up and out her door, another massive branch lay across the remains of her window; the mirror was nowhere to be seen.

Her headlamp was still on her helmet which by some miracle was still on her head. She clicked it on. Trent was still breathing, but out cold. And his arm was at an angle that didn't look good at all.

Twisting herself around, she kicked at what was left of the windshield a few times with her boots until it broke free. The air outside the truck was marginally cooler than inside, which she took as a good sign.

Careful to brace herself so that she didn't fall on Trent, who still wasn't moving, she released her seatbelt. She crawled out to assess the situation. They were at the bottom of a dry ravine that hadn't been on fire. Parts of it now were, though, due to the log that had brought them here and it was bound to get worse shortly.

She leaned back in to extract Trent. Unable to release his seatbelt, she pulled out a knife and cut the straps, but it didn't help much. She weighed about one-twenty-five, and he weighed more like two-twenty-five.

"Great. We're alone, a bajillion miles from no one knows where," she told

Trent's still form. "All the training drills in the world don't make me Supergirl."

"You sure?" A man's voice spoke close behind her.

2

The woman would have fallen over backward if Jess hadn't grabbed her about the waist. She wasn't a bad imitation of Supergirl at all. A blond ponytail hung out below her helmet. She stood two or three inches shorter than his own five-eight—he was still taller than Tom Cruise no matter how much he was teased on the fire line. And she was clad in full fire gear—which was always a turn-on. Firefighting women weren't as rare as they used to be, but ones fighting forest wildfires were still a very rare commodity.

He let go of her as soon as he was sure she had her balance once again.

"No, if I was Supergirl, I'd be able to lift my partner out by myself."

Jess tried not to sigh at the way she said partner. It sounded possessive. Bad luck for him, good luck for the dude still in the truck. Which was now on fire and they'd better get a move on.

He nudged Supergirl out of the way and ducked in to look at the situation. Her partner wasn't pinned but he had a busted arm. No way to assess anything else in this position, not in the time allowed. When Jess tucked the guy's bad arm into his half-open jacket, it didn't even elicit a grunt. Out cold. Jess grabbed the guy's lapels and gave a hard yank. He was big, but he slithered free like a sack of potatoes.

The woman ducked back into the truck through the windshield and emerged moments later with her gloves, a pair of burnover shelters, and the first aid kit. Keeping her head after what must have been a terrifying experience. Full points for that.

Jess had been scouting the edge of the fire. His hotshot crew was up the slope of the ravine trying to cut a line ahead of the blaze and he'd come down just in time to see the engine they'd been waiting for take the hit and tumble down into the ravine.

They'd both dragged the injured driver well clear, then he eyed the truck. There were a lot of supplies on there that they really needed. The flames weren't near the gas tanks yet and it seemed like a reasonable risk.

"Let's do some salvage."

He didn't have to tell her twice. With little ceremony she dropped one shelter and the first aid kit on her prostrate partner's chest. She clipped the other shelter to her belt and followed him back to the truck.

"Grab your PG bag."

"My what?"

"Personal gear."

The fire was bright enough to see the blank look on her face. Right. She probably drove a city engine most of time; she wouldn't know hotshot lingo.

"Food, water, stuff like that."

"Oh," she ducked in and came back out with a small knapsack and a Pulaski fire axe. Okay, not all city. Only wildland firefighters used the tool that was an axe on one side and an adze on the other.

In moments they'd grabbed a five-gallon cube of water and two more of gas for the chainsaws. He snagged a twenty-pound bag of foodstuffs and wished he had time to riffle through more of the doomed engine's lockers. It was trashed anyway, not even worth trying to use its own pump and water supply to put itself out. He'd expected to find two bodies as he approached the cab. And then Supergirl had kicked out the windshield.

She came back out with a stretcher for her partner.

"Let's get clear." In three ferry loads, they put another couple hundred feet between them and the now engulfed engine. They stood in the ashen forest with their salvaged gear and her partner on a stretcher. Jess waited, but even now that they were relatively safe, she didn't slide into shock.

"How bad is the road up to here?"

She looked at him like he was an idiot, which wouldn't surprise anyone, him least of all.

"I mean for an ambulance."

"We don't—" then she looked grim for a moment and glanced down at her partner where he lay strapped into the stretcher. "I don't even know where we are. Visibility was near zero for the last hour."

Jess clicked on the radio, "Candace? Jess here."

"Wondering when you'd get off your lazy ass and check in."

Supergirl had a cute giggle.

"Aww, you missed me. I'm touched. I've got a rollover wildfire engine here at the bottom of the ravine in sector two-six. It's—" there was a loud boom that had both him and Supergirl ducking. She lay over her partner to protect him which was just too sweet for words. "It's toast. That column of flame about a mile to your southeast was one of the gas tanks breaching. Need a medevac and the road is impassable. Got any helos on call?"

"Hold. I'll check."

He turned to Supergirl as she sat back up and began brushing wood chips and other detritus that was falling back down from the explosion off her partner. The engine was a complete loss, but she spared it little more than a glance. He'd seen it before, women so focused on their families that they barely thought about their own safety during evacuations.

"You have a name?"

"Jill Conway-Jones a.k.a. Supergirl."

Sense of humor despite whatever shock she was in. Stretcher boy was one lucky guy; Jess wondered which one of them was Conway and which was Jones. He could see her more clearly now by the light of the burning engine. Seriously lucky guy.

"I'm Jess Monroe. I'm an assistant super on the Leavenworth Interagency Hotshot Crew that's currently up that ridge cutting line. We'll get you and your boyfriend out of here in a minute."

"He's—"

"Jess?" The radio crackled to life sparing him whatever happy domestic story she was going to spill all over him. "Candace here. You're getting lucky tonight, boyo. I've got a Jeannie Clark in Firehawk Oh-Three from MHA heading your way. Give her a beacon. ETA in one minute, she's just finished a dump run and is turning your way. Then get back up here. Please tell me you salvaged some saw fuel."

"Water and food too."

"Love you, Monroe. Swear to god I do."

"You can show me some of that lovin' when I get there. Out." And he began fishing out the infrared beacon. It would show up far brighter in the helicopter pilot's night-vision goggles than a normal flashlight. He hoped that Evan had his radio tuned in for that transmission; Candace's husband was so much fun to poke at. He'd been a hotshot for a year now and married to their super for six months, but it still took him a beat or two to keep up with her. It took all of them that, because Candace rocked the job of leading the team.

The next ten minutes were busy. The helo coming in overhead drowned any conversation beneath the heavy pounding of the big rotors. A guy came down through thick branches on a penetrator winch and helped them hook up the stretcher.

Winch guy took a moment to unsling a camera and snap shots of the burning engine and of Jess and Supergirl double-checking on Trent.

"Be back down for you in a minute," the helo guy shouted to Jill.

"No," she yelled back. "I'm uninjured. I'm sure they can use another firefighter here."

Jess was about to protest.

"I've got my Firefighter I and II, I've been driving wildfire engines for three seasons, and I've got my red card for wildfire." She pointed at the three cubes of fuel and water, "And do you want to carry all those up the hill yourself?"

At forty pounds per cube, he wasn't looking forward to it.

3

"Last chance," the helicopter guy shouted.

Jill waved him aloft, not giving the hotshot a chance to insist. No way was she passing up a chance to work with an IHC crew. Especially not for the sake of Trent who would probably be an engine driver forever. He was headed for what he needed, med care; now it was time to head for what she needed, fire.

In minutes, Trent and the photographer were back aboard the helicopter and the pounding of the rotor blades was fading away.

Funny that the hotshot thought she and Trent were an item.

Jess Monroe was awfully cute. And she'd felt his easy strength when she stumbled and ended up in his arms. Her knees had been shaky from the crash, but after he'd held her, even for that brief moment, she'd felt so much more stable. Too bad he was already taken by his supervisor.

Giving a man too much time to think was never a good idea. So she slipped her Pulaski through the loops on her knapsack… no, her PG bag, and slung it over her shoulders. Then she looped the salvaged food bag over her head.

With a shrug, Jess picked up one of the fuel cubes and the water cube, leaving her the other fuel cube. That was decent of him; five gallons of fuel weighed nine pounds less than the forty-three of the water cubes.

"Ready?" His voice didn't sound at all tight from the heavy load he was now holding.

She scanned the ground, took one last look at the burning engine, trying not to think about the paperwork involved in that loss, and nodded for him to lead the way. She'd miss the engine; it had been a fun machine to drive—had actually made her feel a little like she *was* Supergirl, woman-handling thirteen tons of firefighting beast.

The first hundred feet across the ravine floor went quickly enough. The second hundred, starting up the steep hillside toward the hotshot crew, felt okay too. Then she put her head down and tackled the job of putting one foot in front of the other. In minutes she was drenched in sweat and her arms had started complaining about the load.

Jess led slow and steady, but without stopping and she didn't want to complain, especially as he was carrying thirty more pounds than she was. As they climbed farther into the trees, the orange light from behind faded. A stolen glance showed that they'd climbed a thousand feet or more up from the ravine. The mountains beyond glowed in a hundred shades of red and orange. To the north, flames leapt gold-orange toward the sky. To the south, it was a lower, more sullen burn in deep reds. All else was dark, the forest with night and the sky with thick clouds of smoke. If the helicopter returned, she didn't spot it.

Turning back to the trees, she saw that Jess was well ahead of her now and she did what she could to catch up with him. He had a strong, steady persistence to him.

She wished she had the breath to ask him questions, but she'd left the ability to speak far down the slope.

Instead, she focused her headlamp on the ground in front of her. A simple rhyme formed in her head as she climbed. It so exactly matched the pace of her steps that she was unable to eradicate it.

Jess and Jill went up the hill,
With damned heavy pails of water…

4

Jess had tried to burn her out on the hike
up. He wasn't completely sure of his own
motivations. It wasn't as if there would be
any easy way to evacuate her if she reached
the fire line and then wanted to go home.
The only crews who worked farther from
base on a fire than the hotshots were the
smokejumpers. The smokies went where
there were no roads at all. The hotshots
drove to the end of the road and then
hiked in with nothing but the saws and axes
on their backs. The fact that now they were
only a half mile from a forest road was the

closest they'd been to civilization in five days, having started well to the west.

But every time he glanced back to check on her, Jill Conway-Jones was still there behind him. Sometimes closer, sometimes farther back, and once stopped and turned to stare out at the forest. She hadn't even set down her heavy load, just stood staring out at the wonder of it all.

It was one of the best parts of being a hotshot and it surprised him—and made him like her even more—that she appreciated the land.

The work was brutal, the hours and pay sucked, but to stand out in vast stretches of wilderness and observe the ever-changing landscape was worth almost any price. He hadn't expected some engine driver to understand.

He'd finally turned away from watching Jill watch the fire and continued up the slope. He was always building stupid fantasies in his head and she was just another opportunity make up false dreams.

Jess had never held a fantasy about Candace, or Patsy the team's other assistant super, even before they each had married. But it was still his trademark. Build a ton of stupid dreams and then watch them shatter as reality got in the way. Beautiful blond Supergirl firefighter falls into his arms, sure, but really is partner with someone named Trent. He guessed it was close enough to Clark Kent, but that didn't mean he had to like it. The compound last name put the final stamp on his stupidity.

His legs and arms were burning as he crested another rise and stepped into an unexpected clearing of grass and slash. Three steps later before he could stop himself, he stumbled on a passed-out hotshot and landed full upon him.

"Uh," Evan grunted. "Can't I even get a nap without you crawling in with me? Been waiting on you, Jess. You got any fuel on you?"

Jess rolled off him, too exhausted to speak. The last thousand feet his arms had burned like demons and his attention had tunneled until each step became his whole world. Instead, he thudded his knuckles against one of the cubes.

"Good job, bro," Candace's husband rolled to his feet, something Jess was incapable of at the moment. "Just remember to keep your mind off my woman," Evan paid him back for the earlier tease over the radio with a friendly slap on the shoulder that almost tumbled him back to the lying on the ground. Then Evan headed off in the other direction carrying the fuel cube as if it didn't weigh a thing. He didn't take the water cube. Yet more payback—still worth it.

Now if he could just lie here for a minute until his arms stopped screami—

Jill!

He'd forgotten about her for the last part of the climb. How far behind had he left her? That was rude as hell no matter what he'd been thinking.

He jerked to his feet, spun—and ploughed head on into Jill. Once again he landed on top of a firefighter in the grass.

Jess tried to roll off her but was blocked by the fuel cube she'd been carrying that now lay beside her. He started to roll the other way, but she stopped him.

"You roll onto the food bag after I carried it all this way, you're going to end up being a very dead firefighter."

"Right, sorry." Though it was hard to be completely sorry, lying on top of her, with their faces inches apart and lit by the side glow from their headlamps. He'd been right before how pretty she was. It wasn't just the blond ponytail. She had bright blue eyes and an open face—presently covered with smears of smoke.

"Are you going to be getting up soon or are you just planning to lie there trying to pretend there isn't a fire coming?"

"Uh," he climbed off her and gave her a hand up. "I was just coming back down to—" But she was already here.

"To rescue the poor waif?" She ignored his offer to give her a hand up. "What part of 'I'm a firefighter' didn't you get?"

"The part where you're tougher than I am."

"I'm not tough," she dusted off her Nomex fire-resistant pants and shirt as if he'd somehow dirtied them. Then she fired an absolutely radiant smile at him that almost knocked him to the ground again, "I'm just stubborn as all get out."

5

And if she wasn't, Jill would have had the good sense to have grabbed that helicopter ride and flown out with Trent. It had taken everything she had and more to conquer that ravine's slope with fifty pounds of fuel and food in addition to her own gear. But she'd done it and now that she was here, there wasn't a chance that they were going to find her wanting.

"So," she looked at Jess. He still inspected her wide-eyed as if she'd transported down off an alien ship rather than just battled up a mountain in his silent wake. "Are we good to go?" She didn't even know if she could lift a kitten at this point, never mind a Pulaski.

"Sure," he picked up both his remaining water cube—she'd seen the bobbing light of someone carrying Jess' fuel toward the fire line—and her fuel cube. She was about to call after him that she could carry her own damned fuel, but wasn't sure if she could so she kept her mouth shut. Shouldering the food sack, she followed in his wake.

The night was quiet here.

A chainsaw coughed to life close ahead and then another. In moments they were biting wood.

Okay, it was a relatively quiet night. At least there was no roaring truck engine or even louder fire. The night here was truly dark outside of their helmet lights. The smoke clouds far above glowed the deep red of reflected fire light, but it wasn't bright enough to cast any light over the scene.

What she'd initially taken for a clearing was one end of a fire break. It stretched for a half a mile along the ridgetop. The line had been cut, the branches dragged away, and, once they reached the far side of the cleared line, they were walking on a stretch a dozen yards wide that had been scraped down to deep soil or rock. There were no machines up here, not this high up the mountain. Unbelievably, this had all been done by hand.

Maybe she wasn't ready to be a hotshot.

They reached the far end of the cleared line. Here the chainsaws were hard at work. A line of soot-covered workers followed close behind them dragging away branches.

Jess stopped by a woman wrestling an impossibly large branch into submission.

"Jess! Thanks for the fuel. Chopper's down for the night and they didn't bring any gas in the last supply run."

Jill recognized the voice from the earlier radio exchange. The voice had given no impression of the woman. In person, Candace the team's superintendent looked all-powerful. Smeared with dirt and smoke char, sawdust caught in her hair, she looked like Superwoman making Jill's own Supergirl feel more like Supertoddler.

"I've got a tag-a-long," Jess set down the cubes he was carrying but didn't even have the decency to hug his girlfriend.

Jill moved up beside him and shoved him hard on the shoulder. Unable to step high enough to clear the cube he'd set down, he fell sideways into the cleared dirt.

"I am not a tag-a-long," she practically shouted down at him. "I'm a firefighter." She looked back up at Candace who was watching her with a half smile. "I'm no hotshot, but I've got my red card," Jill said it more quietly this time.

"Well, let's see what kind of a hotshot you make." Candace didn't hold out a hand, leaving Jess to struggle back to his feet as she spoke to him. "She's attached to your hip. Teach her. Safety, procedures, whole thing by the manual. Start with swamping."

"Okay," Jess didn't sound very happy about it, but it was more than Jill had even hoped for—a tryout on a live fire. He headed toward the sound of chainsaws punctuated by the sharp crack of a falling tree.

Candace stopped her before Jill could follow along and looked at her with an intensity that was alarming for a moment, then she smiled brilliantly, her teeth bright in comparison to her char-stained face.

"That one needs a lesson or two in humility. Kick his ass, sister."

Before Jill could respond, Candace had once again clamped onto her branch and was dragging it off into the trees.

For the next twelve hours, she and Jess did just that.

"Swamping. It's called swamping the branches, not dragging."

"Why?"

Jess paused and laughed, making her stumble on the branch he'd been dragging just in front of her. "I haven't a clue. But it's swamping. That much you can trust me on."

As they worked back and forth across the fire line, following behind the sawyers, they spared a some breath to talk. Jess told her about his degree in Psychology.

"Never was much at research and I sure didn't want to spend my life listening to other people's problems. I don't know what I was thinking. It was interesting and

I met some good friends, but being indoors wasn't my idea of living. I met Candace in a coffee shop. She was from a firefighting family and she made it sound so amazing. She and I worked crews all over the west. When she got the call to form up a new team and tapped me for assistant super, it was just about the best day of my life. It was like I really knew I'd done something."

The way he talked about Candace was a curious mixture of humbling and daunting. The more he talked about her, the more imposing the super became. He clearly worshipped the ground she walked on. But it was also a little bit odd. He only spoke of her in relation to firefighting. How she'd done recruitment in a way he'd never seen before. How she kept everyone's spirits up even after a two-day cut on a fire line that was overrun. He never once said anything about their relationship.

"I came from a firefighting family," she told him, but Jill never had much to say beyond that. She came from a line of fire-women. She was the only daughter of two of Seattle's first female fire officers. That she was straight didn't bother her moms; they had made her various boyfriends welcome over the years. And her birth mom's father, Grampa Jones, had been one as well. Jill had served with her parents awhile, but felt overshadowed by them. They were both such strong, outgoing personalities that Jill had feared she was becoming invisible in her own quiet way.

They'd been surprised when she'd signed up for the wildland engine crew. But if they'd been hurt, they didn't show it. Instead, for her birthday they'd given her tuition for both emergency vehicle training and the expensive CDL—the commercial driver's license wasn't required but they had gotten it for her anyway. Neither of which would have saved her from the rolling tree that had wiped out their engine even if she'd been at the wheel.

She kept quiet on the details of her fire-fighting family because she'd learned over the years that most guys didn't understand about growing up with two mothers, so she kept that fact to herself.

She hadn't gone to college. She'd been a Junior Fireman in high school and gone straight into the academy for three months to earn her firefighter certifications. There had never been any question about what she'd do, only what her particular path to fire would be. Listening to Jess Monroe talk about Candace Cantrell was definitely giving her ideas.

6

Jess couldn't get a feel for Jill Conway-Jones. He remembered down at the wrecked engine that she'd been funny. But up here on the line, she was mostly quiet. When she spoke, it was to ask him about hotshotting.

They switched over to grubbing a twenty-foot line, which was just as exciting as it sounded. It was working the dirt with a Pulaski until there was nothing living in a swath that was hopefully wide enough to stop a fire from crossing—not even organic duff was allowed to remain. The cut trees would force the fire down to the ground, the removal of the branches and underbrush would rob it of fuels to slow it further, and the grubbed line would hopefully stop it cold.

But for everything she didn't say, she more than made up for by doing. She'd tirelessly leaned into branches that must have weighed more than she did. And, once she got the proper Pulaski technique, she kept up with him right down the line.

The more he did manage to get from her, the more he cursed the luck of Trent the engine driver, whether he was Conway or Jones. A woman like her didn't come along even every year, never mind every day.

He did finally poke around enough to rediscover her funny side.

"Supergirl is trying to be superhotshot," Jess had forgotten his early nickname for her until they'd worked through the whole night and a dirty, smoking dawn was approaching.

"No, she's actually trying not to be superlame."

"She'd can't be," Jess insisted in between slices with the Pulaski—he had to chop out a stubborn root. "That job description has already been taken by me. Only one allowed per team."

"Fine. You want the title, it's yours," the smile he could hear in her voice through the exhaustion just made him like her all the more. "I'll get myself a t-shirt to prove it. It'll have the red and yellow S on it and then in tiny letters, I'll have it say, '…and, yes, he is with me'."

Almost too exhausted to breathe, she still gave him the energy to laugh.

When sunrise finally did happen, they'd sat on a cut log to rest through a breakfast break of energy bars, an orange, and a canteen of water with electrolyte powder.

"Yum! You hotshots really know how to live the high life."

Jess grimaced, "Just wait until the fire gets here. This has all been prep."

As if in answer to her question, the first air tanker of the morning raced by low overhead, dumping a long line of red retardant on the line of trees beyond the firebreak. Wouldn't do to have some errant spark, of which there would be plenty to hunt down and kill during the height of the battle, ignite the fire beyond the fire line.

7

"How's our tag-a-long doing?" Candace walked up to where she and Jess were still eating on the log. Beside her was one of the sawyers, a big handsome guy she hadn't met yet. Candace put enough sarcasm in her voice that Jill knew she was being teased.

Jess groaned as if wounded to the core and Jill had to fight to suppress a laugh. His constant energy and sense of fun was all that had kept her upright through a brutal night's work.

"I think *I'm* now the tag-a-long," Jess whined like an old man. "Jill doesn't know the meaning of slow down. Picks up technique faster than any recruit who's ever crossed our lines."

"He's been a great teacher," Jill put in. His constant fine-tuning, even long after exhaustion had them both staggering, had revealed a drive for excellence that matched her own and a style of patient teaching that she could only hope to learn some day.

"She learns even faster than you, big guy," he addressed the sawyer.

"No way!" The guy faced her squarely. "Okay, lady. That means it's you and me for the fire. Then we'll see how you do."

Jill couldn't tell if he was teasing or serious. He was an imposing man. Like one of those military clichés with the manly jaw and the broad shoulders.

"Aren't men just the cutest things?" Then Candace pulled him into a kiss.

And not just some friendly peck either.

Jill startled and looked from them to Jess to see how he was taking it. Rather than angry, he looked…

Jealous?

"Come on you two. Do you have to keep proving how happy you are? Get a room, go behind a tree, something."

The big guy broke off and looked down at Candace, "We've got to get him a lady."

Jill was still trying to catch up with what was happening. Jess wasn't with Candace? The big guy was. That explained why he'd only talked about Candace on the fires, because that's what she and Jess did together—team superintendent and assistant. Jill had to sift through all the stories he'd told about their meeting and working together. If they weren't a couple, everything shifted to show his huge respect for a strong woman. She'd thought he was putting his lover up on some silly pedestal, ready to fall.

"How about you, lady?" The big guy looked down at her. "You in the market for a slightly used hotshot? He's kinda scruffy, but we all like him well enough."

"No, she's got a guy, the broken arm we medevaced out last night. Her name's Jill," Jess offered. "Jill, this char-monkey is Evan. But we call him Mud to keep his ego in check." Then he leaned close as if to whisper in confidence, "Doesn't help."

Jill felt cornered until she caught Candace's sly smile. Here were two men who thought that a strong woman was an asset—not just an asset, but absolutely worth seeking out and following. Jill had been raised by two of the strongest women that she'd ever met, ones she'd spent her whole life trying to make proud.

And she'd bet that both of her moms would love these three.

Here they were, three magnificent fire-fighters, standing as friends for a moment in the dawn light before turning to face the approaching flames.

Could there be any place that she'd rather be?

Then she turned to look at Jess. Considerate, passionate…single. He'd spent the whole night telling her about his life and how much he loved what he did and the people he did it with. She'd learned less about some boyfriends in six months than she'd learned about him in the last dozen hours. Jess had blown poor Trent out of the water in the first thirty seconds when he'd caught her and laughed at one of her jokes.

Jill looked at Candace, "Need another hotshot?"

What would have been a ridiculous question a dozen hours ago felt completely normal now.

Candace simply held out a hand and they shook on it. Deal. Done. Yes! She could really get to enjoy working for a woman like her.

She looked back up at Evan.

"Scruffy hotshot slightly used? Might work for me," she poked Jess in the arm as if she was testing a side of beef. "How about this one? Think he's interested?"

She'd never been so forward in her life, but the way his muscles felt, she'd have to do it more often.

Jess was blinking at her, trying just as hard to catch up.

"Trent was my *fire* partner, Jess," she offered the missing clue.

He kept blinking at her in surprise.

"Not the quickest one is he?" Jill glanced up at Candace.

"He's fast enough under normal con-
ditions. But like all the really good ones,"
Candace went up on her toes to kiss Evan
on his cheek, "you can knock them into
stunned puppy land pretty easily."

Jill decided to help Jess along, since she
was the one being forward.

He had called her Supergirl after all.

She leaned over and kissed him.

It took Jess Monroe about two more
seconds and then he caught on very well
indeed. In moments the exhaustion that
had been coursing through her body like
an aching pulse beat was replaced with a
sizzling heat.

"Maybe," Evan drawled out, "we should
get one of the helos to do a water drop on
these two; cool the fire down a bit."

Maybe, Jill thought to herself, but she
didn't think it would make any difference
at all.

About the Author

M. L. Buchman has over 40 novels in print. His military romantic suspense books have been named Barnes & Noble and NPR "Top 5 of the year" and Booklist "Top 10 of the Year." He has been nominated for the Reviewer's Choice Award for "Top 10 Romantic Suspense of 2014" by RT Book Reviews. In addition to romance, he also writes thrillers, fantasy, and science fiction.

In among his career as a corporate project manager he has: rebuilt and single-handed a fifty-foot sailboat, both flown and jumped out of airplanes, designed and built two houses, and bicycled solo around the world.

He is now making his living as a full-time writer on the Oregon Coast with his beloved wife. He is constantly amazed at what you can do with a degree in Geophysics. You may keep up with his writing *and get exclusively free short stories* by subscribing to his newsletter at: www. mlbuchman.com.

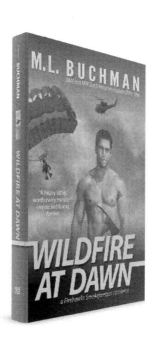

Wildfire at Dawn
(Book #1 of the Firehawks
Smokejumpers trilogy
—an excerpt)

Mount Hood Aviation's lead smokejumper Johnny Akbar Jepps rolled out of his lower bunk careful not to bang his head on the upper. Well, he tried to roll out, but every muscle fought him, making it more a crawl than a roll. He checked the clock on his phone. Late morning.

He'd slept twenty of the last twenty-four hours and his body felt as if he'd spent the entire time in one position. The coarse plank flooring had been worn smooth by thousands of feet hitting exactly this same spot year in and year out for decades. He managed to stand upright…then he felt it, his shoulders and legs screamed.

Oh, right.

The New Tillamook Burn. Just about the nastiest damn blaze he'd fought in a decade of jumping wildfires. Two hundred thousand acres—over three hundred square miles—of rugged Pacific Coast Range forest, poof! The worst forest fire in a decade for the Pacific Northwest, but they'd killed it off without a single fatality or losing a single town. There'd been a few bigger ones, out in the flatter eastern part of Oregon state. But that much area— mostly on terrain too steep to climb even when it wasn't on fire—had been a horror.

Akbar opened the blackout curtain and winced against the summer brightness of blue sky and towering trees that lined the firefighter's camp. Tim was gone from the upper bunk, without kicking Akbar on his way out. He must have been as hazed out as Akbar felt.

He did a couple of side stretches and could feel every single minute of the eight straight days on the wildfire to contain the bastard, then the excruciating nine days more to convince it that it was dead enough to hand off to a Type II incident mop-up crew. Not since his beginning days on a hotshot crew had he spent seventeen days on a single fire.

And in all that time nothing more than catnaps in the acrid safety of the "black"—the burned-over section of a fire, black with char and stark with no hint of green foliage. The mop-up crews would be out there for weeks before it was dead past restarting, but at least it was truly done in. That fire wasn't merely contained; they'd killed it bad.

Yesterday morning, after demobilizing, his team of smokies had pitched into their bunks. No wonder he was so damned sore.

His stretches worked out the worst of the kinks but he still must be looking like an old man stumbling about.

He looked down at the sheets. Damn it. They'd been fresh before he went to the fire, now he'd have to wash them again. He'd been too exhausted to shower before sleeping and they were all smeared with the dirt and soot that he could still feel caking his skin. Two-Tall Tim, his number two man and as tall as two of Akbar, kinda, wasn't in his bunk. His towel was missing from the hook.

Shower. Shower would be good. He grabbed his own towel and headed down the dark, narrow hall to the far end of the bunk house. Every one of the dozen doors of his smoke teams were still closed, smokies still sacked out. A glance down another corridor and he could see that at least a couple of the Mount Hood Aviation helicopter crews were up, but most still had closed doors with no hint of light from open curtains sliding under them. All of MHA had gone above and beyond on this one.

"Hey, Tim." Sure enough, the tall Eurasian was in one of the shower stalls, propped up against the back wall letting the hot water stream over him.

"Akbar the Great lives," Two-Tall sounded half asleep.

"Mostly. Doghouse?" Akbar stripped down and hit the next stall. The old plywood dividers were flimsy with age and gray with too many showers. The Mount Hood Aviation firefighters' Hoodie One base camp had been a kids' summer camp for decades. Long since defunct, MHA had taken it over and converted the playfields into landing areas for their helicopters, and regraded the main road into a decent airstrip for the spotter and jump planes.

"Doghouse? Hell, yeah. I'm like ten thousand calories short." Two-Tall found some energy in his voice at the idea of a trip into town.

The Doghouse Inn was in the nearest town. Hood River lay about a half hour down the mountain and had exactly what they needed: smokejumper-sized portions and a very high ratio of awesomely fit

young women come to windsurf the
Columbia Gorge. The Gorge, which
formed the Washington and Oregon
border, provided a fantastically target-rich
environment for a smokejumper too long
in the woods.

"You're too tall to be short of anything,"
Akbar knew he was being a little slow to
reply, but he'd only been awake for minutes.

"You're like a hundred thousand calories
short of being even a halfway decent size,"
Tim was obviously recovering faster than
he was.

"Just because my parents loved me
instead of tying me to a rack every night
ain't my problem, buddy."

He scrubbed and soaped and scrubbed
some more until he felt mostly clean.

"I'm telling you, Two-Tall. Whoever
invented the hot shower, that's the dude we
should give the Nobel prize to."

"You say that every time."

"You arguing?"

He heard Tim give a satisfied groan as
some muscle finally let go under the steamy
hot water. "Not for a second."

Akbar stepped out and walked over to the line of sinks, smearing a hand back and forth to wipe the condensation from the sheet of stainless steel screwed to the wall. His hazy reflection still sported several smears of char.

"You so purdy, Akbar."

"Purdier than you, Two-Tall." He headed back into the shower to get the last of it.

"So not. You're jealous."

Akbar wasn't the least bit jealous. Yes, despite his lean height, Tim was handsome enough to sweep up any ladies he wanted.

But on his own, Akbar did pretty damn well himself. What he didn't have in height, he made up for with a proper smokejumper's muscled build. Mixed with his tan-dark Indian complexion, he did fine.

The real fun, of course, was when the two of them went cruising together. The women never knew what to make of the two of them side by side. The contrast kept them off balance enough to open even more doors.

He smiled as he toweled down. It also didn't hurt that their opening answer to "what do you do" was "I jump out of planes to fight forest fires."

Worked every damn time. God he loved this job.

# # #

The small town of Hood River, a winding half-an-hour down the mountain from the MHA base camp, was hopping. Mid-June, colleges letting out. Students and the younger set of professors high-tailing it to the Gorge. They packed the bars and breweries and sidewalk cafes. Suddenly every other car on the street had a wind-surfing board tied on the roof.

The snooty rich folks were up at the historic Timberline Lodge on Mount Hood itself, not far in the other direction from MHA. Down here it was a younger, thrill seeker set and you could feel the energy.

There were other restaurants in town that might have better pickings, but the Doghouse Inn was MHA tradition and it was a good luck charm—no smokie in his right mind messed with that. This was the bar where all of the MHA crew hung out.

It didn't look like much from the outside, just a worn old brick building beaten by the Gorge's violent weather. Aged before its time, which had been long ago.

But inside was awesome. A long wooden bar stretched down one side with a half-jillion microbrew taps and a small but well-stocked kitchen at the far end. The dark wood paneling, even on the ceiling, was barely visible beneath thousands of pictures of doghouses sent from patrons all over the world. Miniature dachshunds in ornately decorated shoeboxes, massive Newfoundlands in backyard mansions that could easily house hundreds of their smaller kin, and everything in between. A gigantic Snoopy atop his doghouse in full Red Baron fighting gear dominated the far wall. Rumor said Shulz himself had been here two owners before and drawn it.

Tables were grouped close together, some for standing and drinking, others for sitting and eating.

"Amy, sweetheart!" Two-Tall called out as they entered the bar. The perky redhead came out from behind the bar to receive a hug from Tim. Akbar got one in turn, so he wasn't complaining. Cute as could be and about his height; her hugs were better than taking most women to bed. Of course, Gerald the cook and the bar's co-owner was big enough and strong enough to squish either Tim or Akbar if they got even a tiny step out of line with his wife. Gerald was one amazingly lucky man.

Akbar grabbed a Walking Man stout and turned to assess the crowd. A couple of the air jocks were in. Carly and Steve were at a little table for two in the corner, obviously not interested in anyone's company but each others. Damn, that had happened fast. New guy on the base swept up one of the most beautiful women on the planet. One of these days he'd have to ask Steve how he'd done that. Or maybe not. It looked like they were settling in for the long haul; the big "M" was so not his own first choice.

Carly was also one of the best FBANs in the business. Akbar was a good Fire Behavior Analyst, had to be or he wouldn't have made it to first stick—lead smokie of the whole MHA crew. But Carly was

something else again. He'd always found
the Flame Witch, as she was often called,
daunting and a bit scary besides; she knew
the fire better than it did itself. Steve had
latched on to one seriously driven lady.
More power to him.

The selection of female tourists was
especially good today, but no other smokies
in yet. They'd be in soon enough…most of
them had groaned awake and said they were
coming as he and Two-Tall kicked their
hallway doors, but not until they'd been on
their way out—he and Tim had first pick.
Actually some of the smokies were coming,
others had told them quite succinctly where
they could go—but hey, jumping into fiery
hell is what they did for a living anyway, so
no big change there.

A couple of the chopper pilots had
nailed down a big table right in the middle of
the bustling seating area: Jeannie, Mickey,
and Vern. Good "field of fire" in the
immediate area.

He and Tim headed over, but Akbar
managed to snag the chair closest to the
really hot lady with down-her-back curling

dark-auburn hair at the next table over—set just right to see her profile easily. Hard shot, sitting there with her parents, but damn she was amazing. And if that was her mom, it said the woman would be good looking for a long time to come.

Two-Tall grimaced at him and Akbar offered him a comfortable "beat out your ass" grin. But this one didn't feel like that. Maybe it was the whole parental thing. He sat back and kept his mouth shut.

He made sure that Two-Tall could see his interest. That made Tim honor bound to try and cut Akbar out of the running.

# # #

Laura Jenson had spotted them coming into the restaurant. Her dad was only moments behind.

"Those two are walking like they just climbed off their first-ever horseback ride."

She had to laugh, they did. So stiff and awkward they barely managed to move upright. They didn't look like first-time windsurfers, aching from the unexpected workout. They'd also walked in like they thought they were two gifts to god, which was even funnier. She turned away to avoid laughing in their faces. Guys who thought like that rarely appreciated getting a reality check.

A couple minutes later, at a nod from her dad, she did a careful sideways glance. Sure enough, they'd joined in with a group of friends who were seated at the next table behind her. The short one, shorter than she was by four or five inches, sat to one side. He was doing the old stare without staring routine, as if she were so naïve as to not recognize it. His ridiculously tall companion sat around the next turn of the table to her other side.

Then the tall one raised his voice enough to be heard easily over her dad's story about the latest goings-on at the local drone manufacturer. His company was the first one to be certified by the FAA for limited testing on wildfire and search-and-rescue overflights. She wanted to hear about it, but the tall guy had a deep voice that carried as if he were barrel-chested rather than pencil thin.

"Hell of fire, wasn't it? Where do you think we'll be jumping next?"

Smokies. Well, maybe they had some right to arrogance, but it didn't gain any ground with her.

"Please make it a small one," a woman who Laura couldn't see right behind her chimed in. "I wouldn't mind getting to sleep at least a couple times this summer if I'm gonna be flying you guys around."

Laura tried to listen to her dad, but the patter behind her was picking up speed.

Another guy, "Yeah, know what you mean, Jeannie. I caught myself flying along trying to figure out how to fit crows and Stellar jays with little belly tanks to douse the flames. Maybe get a turkey vulture with a Type I heavy load classification."

"At least you weren't knocked down," Jeannie again. Laura liked her voice; she sounded fun. "Damn tree took out my rotor. They got it aloft, but maintenance hasn't signed it off for fire yet. They better have it done before the next call." A woman who knew no fear—or at least knew about getting back up on the horse.

A woman who flew choppers; that was kind of cool actually. Laura had thought about smokejumping, but not very hard. She enjoyed being down in the forest too much. She'd been born and bred to be a guide. And her job at Timberline Lodge let her do a lot of that.

Dad was working on the search-and-rescue testing. Said they could find a human body heat signature, even in deep trees.

"Hey," Laura finally managed to drag her attention wholly back to her parents. "If you guys need somewhere to test them, I'd love to play. As the Lodge's activities director, I'm down rivers, out on lakes, and leading mountain hikes on most days. All with tourists. And you know how much trouble they get into."

Mom laughed, she knew exactly what her daughter meant. Laura had come by the trade right down the matrilineal line. Grandma had been a fishing and hunting tour guide out of Nome, Alaska back when a woman had to go to Alaska to do more than be a teacher or nurse. Mom had done the same until she met a man from the lower forty-eight who promised they could ride horses almost year-round in Oregon. Laura had practically grown up on horseback, leading group rides deep into the Oregon Wilderness first with her mom and, by the time she was in her mid-teens, on her own.

They chatted about the newest drone technology for a while.

The guy with the big, deep voice finally faded away, one less guy to worry about hitting on her. But out of her peripheral vision, she could still see the other guy, the short one with the tan-dark skin, tight curly black hair, and shoulders like Atlas.

He'd teased the tall guy as they sat down and then gone silent. Not quite watching her; the same way she was not quite watching him.

Her dad missed what was going on, but her mom's smile was definitely giving her shit about it.

Available at fine retailers everywhere

More information at:
www.mlbuchman.com

Other works by M.L. Buchman

Angelo's Hearth
Where Dreams are Born
Where Dreams Reside
Maria's Christmas Table
Where Dreams Unfold
Where Dreams Are Written

Deities Anonymous
Cookbook from Hell: Reheated
Saviors 101

Thrillers
Swap Out!
One Chef!
Two Chef!

SF/F Titles
Nara
Monk's Maze

20636867R00043

Printed in Great Britain
by Amazon